PRESENTED BY:

Van Wert Lions Club

When Anju Loved Being an Elephant

Wendy Henrichs

illustrated by John Butler

PUBLISHED BY SLEEPING BEAR PRESS

Sleeping Bear Press™

315 East Eisenhower Parkway, Suite 200
Ann Arbor, MI 48108
www.sleepingbearpress.com

© 2011 Sleeping Bear Press, a part of Cengage Learning.

10 9 8 7 6 5 4 3 2 1

Library of Congress Cataloging-in-Publication Data

Henrichs, Wendy.
When Anju loved being an elephant / written by Wendy Henrichs ; illustrated by John Butler.
p. cm.
Summary: Anju the Asian elephant recalls her childhood in Sumatra,
and the American circuses and zoos in which she toiled for fifty years,
when she is loaded into a trailer truck and taken to a sanctuary.
Includes advice on helping elephants and "Elephant Q&A".
ISBN 978-1-58536-533-3
1. Asiatic elephant--Juvenile fiction. [1. Asiatic elephant--Fiction. 2. Elephants--Fiction.
3. Animal sanctuaries--Fiction.]
I. Butler, John, 1952- ill. II. Title.
PZ10.3.H398Whe 2011
[E]--dc22
2010053708

Printed by China Translation & Printing Services Limited,
Guangdong Province,China. 1st printing.   04/2011

To my dear family–Mark, Miles, and Eli

Wendy

To Margaret

John

S he first came to America as a wee calf of only five years, bought and sold as a circus elephant. Although she's traveled untold miles since, her home these last fifteen years has been this small patch of zoo grass.

Now, she's on the move again.

Her *mahout*, or elephant caretaker, Vincent, chains her leg and asks her to walk up a ramp into a trailer truck. Even with her deep trust of Vincent, she holds fast, not budging her eight thousand pounds.

"C'mon, Anju," he coaxes, tugging at the chain. "Ease in, old girl. That's right, Anju … that's my girl!"

In his outstretched hand, he offers slices of oranges, her favorite food. He knows he can sway her with that sweet, tangy fruit.

From the front of the semitruck, Vincent reassures her in his velvety voice, "Don't worry, Anj. You're goin' to a better place."

Through the trailer window, she sees the tall, spindly Carolina pines, rooted in their rusty-red soil, for the last time. Although old and tired now, she remembers. She remembers trees like these on her childhood island of Sumatra.

There, in Indonesia, she was born some fifty long years ago. And there, she and her best friend, Lali, would give themselves glorious backrubs against the enormous orange-barked pines of their jungle.

She often thinks of Lali. *Is she still there–so many oceans away, so many years away–or was she taken, too?*

Anju was born under the star-blazoned night sky of Sumatra, then Lali, one night later. The matriarch, the biggest, strongest, and oldest female of their herd, welcomed them, caressing their heads and ears gently … gently … in her regal fashion.

Ears waving and always trunk-to-trunk, Anju and Lali would travel and eat … travel and eat … with their mothers and herd-family for eighteen hours a day, the soft jungle earth beneath their round feet. As the two friends romped and rolled in rivers and mud holes, their dear mothers taught them the many uses of their amazing trunks:

a *hose* to drink and spray with,

a *nose* to smell and trumpet-talk with,

a *vacuum* for sucking up seeds and small fruits with, and

a *strong arm* for picking up tiny things and big things.

The rhythmic, lapping waters of the surrounding Indian Ocean and South China Sea were their island lullaby. Closing their long-lashed eyelids and lying together with their families, Anju and Lali slept in the tall, ticklish grasses, heartbeat-to-heartbeat.

Anju remembers those childhood days when she loved being an elephant.

    As she stands on the hard floor of the trailer truck, the chain *clinks* and *clanks* at her ankle. From the trailer window, Anju sees cars whiz by on the highway.

    She remembers the clown cars in the circus. Round-and-round, round-and-round they'd spin, a dizzying mix of color and noise in the grandstand ring.

In that new and strange circus-world, she remembers the constant travel from town to town in boxcars and trailers. She remembers long hours chained to one spot. And she remembers learning the circus tricks. Some trainers were kind, but others used the bull-hook.

Far away from her mother and Lali, Anju searched and searched for a new kind of family, one that spoke her language—the language humans could not hear—low rumblings from deep inside their trunks, words shared to soothe their elephant souls.

But every time Anju made a new elephant friend, they were SOLD! to another circus, and she would once again stand alone, just as she did at the port of Sumatra all those years ago.

Yes, Anju remembers her circus days when she searched for elephant friends.

And now, where is Vincent taking her? Another circus? She's too old for whips and tricks and rolling across America. Another zoo? Vincent has cared for her well, but it was a solitary place with no other elephants to befriend her for all those years.

Anju's heart has been lonely, although her mother and Lali have always lived in it.

The semitrailer jostles and sways ... jostles and sways. Vincent almost sings to her: "Don't you worry, Anj. You'll always be my girl! You're goin' to a better place now! No more worries."

A day's journey later, the semitruck finally stops … far from her birthplace in Sumatra, far from the circus big top, and far from the zoo she has left with Vincent.

Vincent tugs at her chain, luring her down the ramp with more orange slices. A woman calls, "Hello, Anju! Welcome!" She leads Anju into her own barn stall where bananas, oranges, broccoli, and carrots brim over a basket, waiting just for her.

The smells of elephants are all around.

Will they be friendly?

CLANK!

Vincent drops her chain to the ground and hugs her for the last time, saying,
"Anju, I know you'll be happy here." Anju touches him with her trunk. Wiping tears
from his eyes, he says, "Goodbye, Anju. I'll miss you, girl, but now you're free.
Finally free! You'll see, Anj, it'll be like going home again.
In the wild. Where you came from."

Vincent has gone. The woman remains in
her stall, offering fruit and talking to her.
She is her new *mahout* now.

An elephant, Elsa, comes to meet Anju.

Will she be kind?

Elsa approaches slowly. The two rumble and talk, sniffing the air between them with open mouths. They touch gently with their trunks.

Elsa is kind!

Even with Elsa's tenderness, Anju backs to the corner of her stall, leery as the gate opens, inviting her to explore the long-stretching fields of never-ending green. She has been confined and chained to small spaces for nearly fifty years. This openness is too large, too looming.

Elsa snorts encouraging rumbles to Anju.

The woman and others look on, wondering what Anju will do.
Finally, one step …

two steps …

Anju slowly …

slowly … allows Elsa to lead her out of the stall!
Walking shoulder-to-shoulder, they explore Anju's new home.

Elsa showers Anju's skin with a protective spray of dust.
Ears waving, Anju repays her new friend.

In a pond, they splash, shower, and loll.

Anju leans her head toward Elsa and is hugged back.

To dry off, they walk to a sunny pasture in the tall, ticklish grass
where other elephants rest, and there Anju sleeps, heartbeat-to-heartbeat,
with not only Elsa, but an entire herd of elephants!

Anju knows this is a place where she can be free—truly free—

and where she will always love being an elephant.

Elephant Facts

Q: **Where do elephants live in the wild?**

A: Although elephant habitats and populations are dwindling, wild elephants are still found in Africa, India, and parts of Indonesia. They are highly social and intelligent animals that live in closely knit families (herds) of six to twelve elephants.

Q: **What is an elephant's greatest threat?**

A: Only elephant calves are threatened by predators—lions, leopards, cheetahs, and hyenas in Africa and tigers in India and Indonesia. An elephant's main threat is humans. People kill them to acquire their tusks for ivory (poaching). Farmers, whose crop land has encroached upon elephant habitats, attempt to control elephant populations through killing (culls) in order to protect crops.

Q: **What is the lifespan of an elephant?**

A: In the wild, elephants can live up to 60–70 years. In captivity, their life expectancy lowers to 50–60 years.

Q: **What do elephants eat and how much do they drink?**

A: In the wild, elephants may spend eighteen hours a day roaming to find enough leaves, branches, bark, grasses, roots, and fruits, up to 300 pounds a day. A calf will nurse until it is four or five years old. At age two, grasses are introduced. Adult elephants will drink 45 gallons of water per day.

Q: How many muscles does an elephant's trunk have?

A: An elephant's trunk contains over 40,000 muscles and is vital for acquiring food, whether for reaching leaves high in the treetops or for sucking up water to fill their mouths. Although a calf can walk within one hour of birth, it will not master the use of its trunk for several months.

Q: Why do elephants toss dirt on themselves?

A: In Greek, *pachyderm* means "thick-skinned," and, although an elephant's skin is thick (one inch thick on its back), it is very sensitive to sunburn and bug bites. The dirt acts as a protectant.

Q: Do elephants really have good memories?

A: Yes! The old saying, "An elephant never forgets," is true. There are known instances of elephants who have not seen each other for decades and, when reunited, show intense signs of recognition and display a deep bond from their shared past.

Q: Can elephants really talk to each other?

A: Yes, by using elephant *infrasound*, the low frequency rumblings we humans cannot hear. Scientists believe that our ears can only pick up one-third of an elephant's vocalizations and that the two-thirds we can't hear can be heard by elephants up to five miles away.

Q: What are some ways that elephants have shown caring or empathetic behaviors?

A: Elephants have a deep capacity for empathy. In their herds, family members help mothers care for their young, and if a mother should perish, it is not unusual for other members of the herd to adopt an orphaned elephant. When a member of a herd is injured or sick, elephants will stand beside them to help them walk, or will bring food to a weak member who is healing. Elephants also display funeral rituals for family members who have passed, intensely mourning them.

Although Anju is a fictional elephant, her story rings true for the majority of elephants in captivity. Anju's retirement to a wonderful elephant sanctuary is the outcome desired to bring dignity and respect to all captive elephants.

Ways You Can Help Elephants

1.) Encourage your parents not to purchase ivory.

2.) Encourage family vacations that avoid elephant performance. For international listings of animal-free circuses, search bornfreeusa.org and circuses.com.

3.) Always report animal cruelty or neglect to adults and your local humane society.

4.) Donations and letter-writing campaigns are two of the ways you can help with these reputable elephant organizations:

   The Elephant Sanctuary (elephants.com)

   HelpElephants.com, associated with In Defense of Animals (idausa.org)

   Born Free Foundation (bornfreeusa.org)

   World Society for the Protection of Animals (wspa-usa.org)

   People for the Ethical Treatment of Animals (peta.org)